Whatever Happened to Humpty Dumpty?

And Other Surprising Sequels to Mother Goose Rhymes

by David T. Greenberg

Illustrated by S. D. Schindler

Little, Brown and Company
Boston New York London

To Sharon, my Goose
most beautiful and precious
— D.T.G.

Text copyright © 1999 by David T. Greenberg
Illustrations copyright © 1999 by S. D. Schindler

First Edition

Library of Congress Cataloging-in-Publication Data

Greenberg, David (David T.)
    Whatever happened to Humpty Dumpty? : and other surprising sequels to
Mother Goose rhymes / by David T. Greenberg ; illustrated by S. D. Schindler. —
1st ed.
        p.   cm.
    Summary: Humorous verses are added to traditional Mother Goose rhymes.
    ISBN 0-316-32767-0
    1. Mother Goose — Parodies, imitations, etc.   2. Children's poetry,
American.   3. Nursery rhymes, American.   [1. American poetry.   2. Nursery
rhymes.]   I. Schindler, S. D., ill.   II. Mother Goose.   III. Title.
PS3557.R37828W48   1998
811'.54 — dc21   97-14173
                        10 9 8 7 6 5 4 3 2 1

                                SC

                        Printed in Hong Kong

Humpty Dumpty

Humpty Dumpty sat on a wall,
Humpty Dumpty had a great fall;
All the king's horses and all the king's men
Couldn't put Humpty together again.

When Humpty Dumpty broke,
All that was left was his yolk.
It was sticky and yellow and wiggled like Jell-O
If you gave it the teensiest poke.

So all the king's horses and all the king's men,
The king, the queen, the royal hen,
The regal dog, the imperial mole
Scooped Humpty Dumpty into a bowl.

Gently they carried him back to the castle,
For his yolk was rather tender.
Then they all grabbed the bowl (including the mole)
And poured him into a blender.

"Omelets with parsley, omelets with cheese!"
Screamed the king as loud as he could.
"Omelets with garlic and fresh garden peas,"
Yelled the queen, "are equally good!"

"Omelets with barley and clover and hay!"
All the king's horses snorted.
"Omelets with beetles and worms in decay!"
The mole boldly retorted.

Then they gleefully turned to the blender.
The king plugged it in, he did.
He turned it on full power
But forgot to put on the lid.

Humpty Dumpty sat on a wall,
Humpty Dumpty had a great fall.
And I'm very sad to tell you, my dear,
That now they'll be cleaning him up for a year.

Jack

Jack be nimble,
Jack be quick,
Jack jumped over the candlestick.

Jack be quick,
Jack be faster,
Jack be — oh, my gosh — disaster!

Jack tripped over the candlestick,
Caught fire in a flash.
Now all that's left of Jack
Is a little bit of ash.*

* They buried him in his socks.
   He's now a Jack-in-the-box.

Jerry Hall

Jerry Hall, he was so small,
A rat could eat him, hat and all.

Drat!
He was swallowed by a rat.
Now there isn't any question
He will suffer in digestion.

Five Toes

This little piggy went to market,
This little piggy stayed home,
This little piggy had roast beef,
This little piggy had none,
This little piggy said, "Wee, wee!
I can't find my way home."

"Wee wee wee" said he, said he,
"Wee wee wee wee wee
P-poor lost pig I am, I am,
P-pitiful pork chop me."

"I'll help you," said a lady bent
(Really a wolf in disguise).
"Come with me, my child.
Let auntie dry your eyes."

"Th-th-thank you," squealed the piggy lost.
"You're v-very very nice.
P-p-please c-call my mommy
And she'll be here in a trice."

And the wolf pretended to call his mom
And pretended to be lovin',
And she tucked him into bed
And quietly lit the oven.

Then she went and got an ax
For chopping off his head,
But when she returned to his room,
He wasn't in his bed.

He wasn't in the closet,
He wasn't in the foyer,
But when she opened the cupboard,
Standing there before her

Were five midget pigs,
Wearing superhero suits,
Each one in a mask
And shiny leather boots.

The Fabulous Piggies Five,
Protectors of all swines.
"Mrs. Wolf, the time has come
To answer for your crimes."

"You've beaten us and eaten us,
You've terrorized our town,
You've followed us and swallowed us,
You've blown our houses down.

"What do you say, Mrs. Wolf?"
Demanded the pig police.
"Speak your last words now
Or forever hold your peace."

"It's not my fault," howled Mrs. Wolf.
"Us wolves, we must eat meat.
If I didn't eat a pig,
What else could I eat?

"I guess I could eat rabbits
Or cows or marmoset,
But they wouldn't like it either
And would also be upset.

"So kill me if you like,
Please do not delay,
But I had no choice at all—
I'm innocent, I say."

"Oh, we don't intend to kill you,"
Spoke the Piggies Five.
"We're not as cruel as you.
We're taking you alive."

So they put her into paw cuffs,
Tied square knots in her tail,
And then they hauled her off
To their wicked-wolfy jail.

Now she works there on a chain gang,
Pulverizing stones
That the pigs all use for building
Wolf-resistant homes.

Old Mother Goose

Old Mother Goose, when
She wanted to wander,
Would ride through the air
On a very fine gander.

They both went
Up to heaven
After colliding with a

747.

It's Raining

It's raining, it's pouring,
The old man is snoring.
He went to bed
And bumped his head
And couldn't wake up in the morning.

They tried to wake him with smelling salts,
They tried with cod-liver oil,
Which they poured each day on his pillow
(Until it started to spoil).

They tried to wake him with electrical eels,
They tried with magical fires,
They tried by plucking his nostril hairs
One at a time with pliers.

They tried to wake him with Eskimo kisses,
They tried to wake him with spears,
They tried to wake him with baby pigs
That they hung from the lobes of his ears.

At last they called in an expert
And this is what she said:
"Why, this man's been dead for twenty years —
Ever since bumping his head."

There Was an Old Woman

There was an old woman who lived in a shoe;
She had so many children she didn't know what to do.
She gave them some broth without any bread,
Then whipped them all soundly and put them to bed.

Did things work out for that mom and her kids?
Sadly, the answer is no, ma'am,
For a giant stuck his foot in the shoe
And now they're all in a toe jam.

Baby Dolly

Hush, baby, my dolly, I pray you, don't cry,
And I'll give you some bread and some milk by and by,
Or perhaps you like custard or maybe a tart—
Then to either you're welcome, with all my heart.

"I don't want bread—
Custard, yuck.
Milk and tarts
Totally suck.

"This dolly don't want
Your homemade jam,
Your fat-free turkey,
Fancy ham.

"Doritos and Cool Whip—
    that's what I want—
French fries, melted Velveeta.
This dolly wants Godiva chocolate
(The only brand I'll eat-a).

"Give me popcorn drenched in butter,
Give me Reese's Pieces
And really fatty pork chops
Gurgling in greases.

"And give it to me right away—
Hurry up, you twit,
And serve it on a silver platter
Or this doll will throw a fit!"

Little King Boggen

Little King Boggen, he built a fine hall.
Piecrust and pastry crust, that was the wall;
The windows were made of black puddings and white,
And slated with pancakes — you ne'er saw the like!

There were gables made of gummy worms,
Turrets, buttered toast.
The bathtubs were bananas
The rugs were well-done roast.

King Boggen's hall was scrumptious,
Mouthwatering, incredible,
Outside-out and inside-in
Absolutely edible.

In fact, King Boggen's hall
(Though you might believe I jest)
Was featured in a magazine:
Royal House Digest.

And that's, of course, where Curly-locks
Read about his shack.
And she quickly snorted over
For a deadly snack attack.

King Boggen fought her valiantly
With missiles made from mustard,
Torpedoes made from taffy;
He catapulted custard.

He bombed her with baloney,
He blasted her with juice,
He shot at her with sugar,
But it wasn't any use.

For Curly-locks ate his house up,
Battlements to dungeons
(With a bit of sliced tomato,
Mayonnaise, and unjions).

Then she blasted out a belch
Like a blown-up battleship
And very, very daintily
Dabbed her dainty lip.

The Pumpkin Eater

Peter, Peter, pumpkin eater,
Had a wife and couldn't keep her;
He put her in a pumpkin shell
And there he kept her very well.

But Peter's wife grew bored
Living in that pumpkin.
Living in a gourd
Made her such a grumpkin.

So her put her in a melon,
Hoping for the best,
But Peter's wife grew melancholy,
Terribly depressed.

He put her in a coconut,
Then he put her in a lentil
(It was so cramped inside that lentil
That it almost drove her mental).

And he was just about to stick her
In a hollow loaf of bread
When she grabbed him by the collar
And stuck *him* in instead!

(She waved to him farewell
And there she kept him very well.)

Three Wise Men of Gotham

Three wise men of Gotham
Went to sea in a bowl;
If the bowl had been stronger
My song had been longer.

Their wives tried to rescue them
And followed them out in a platter.
Now there are several sharks
Who are happier and fatter.

Jack and Jill

Jack and Jill went up the hill
To fetch a pail of water;
Jack fell down and broke his crown,
And Jill came tumbling after.

Oh, Jill and Jack Malone
Were incredibly accident-prone.
You'd hardly believe the smacks and dents
They got from all their accidents.

Their mom sent Jill to market
For soda, snacks, and beer.
She fell into a freezer case,
Had frostbite for a year.

"Go upstairs," their father said,
"And quickly clean your room."
Jack tripped over a shoe on the floor
And poked out his eye with a broom.

Finally, they fell in the toilet
And quite inadvertently
Pulled the handle down
And flushed themselves out to sea.

The Crooked Sixpence

There was a crooked man, and he went a crooked mile;
He found a crooked sixpence beside a crooked stile;
He bought a crooked cat, which caught a crooked mouse,
And they all lived together in a crooked little house.

With the crooked moon in the crooked sky
And a crooked gleam in their crooked eye,
They crept from their crooked house —

The crooked man and the crooked cat,
Crookedly wearing a crooked hat,
And the utterly crooked mouse.

They crookedly crept down the crooked street
On the crooked toes of their crooked feet,
The three of them crookedly hopin'
For a crooked window open.

They eventually found one, and crookedly entered
The house of Mr. Bunny,
And while Mr. Bunny crookedly slept,
They crookedly stole his money.

They were crookedly caught the very next day
And put in a crooked jail.
"Why did you steal my money?"
Wailed Mr. Cottontail.

And the crooked man and the cat and mouse
All crookedly traded looks.
"Because," they said to the rabbit,
"The three of us are crooks."

Sing a Song of Sixpence

Sing a song of sixpence,
A pocket full of rye,
Four-and-twenty blackbirds
Baked in a pie.

When the pie was opened,
The birds began to sing.
Was not that a dainty dish
To set before a king?

The king was in his counting house,
Counting out his money;
The queen was in the parlor,
Eating bread and honey.

The maid was in the garden,
Hanging out the clothes,
When down came a blackbird
And snapped off her nose.

They raced the maid to the hospital,
Where they replaced her nose with a pea.
The maid, however, objected:
"That pea just isn't me."

So they traded the pea for a giant squid,
Truly repulsive to touch.
Said the maid, "I just adore it,
But he squirms a little too much."

These doctors wouldn't give up;
They replaced the squid with a fork.
The maid screamed out in horror,
"It makes me look like a dork!"

They changed the fork for a Ping-Pong paddle
Made out of rubber and wood.
"I want my nose to be great," said the maid.
"This is merely good."

"A great nose," exclaimed the doctors,
"A glorious, glorious nose —
You should have said in the first place
That you wanted one of those."

And to her face they attached
An entire continent,
And the maid continentedly sighed,
"That's exactly what I meant."

Oh, the king and queen have money and honey,
But both heave jealous sighs,
For their maid has her very own continent
Right before her eyes.

Mary's Lamb

Mary had a little lamb,
Its fleece was white as snow,
And everywhere that Mary went
The lamb was sure to go.

It followed her to school one day,
Which was against the rule.
It made the children laugh and play
To see a lamb in school.

And so the teacher turned it out,
But still it lingered near
And waited patiently about
Till Mary did appear.

"What makes the lamb love Mary so?"
The eager children cry.
"Why, Mary loves the lamb, you know,"
The teacher did reply.

But what the teacher didn't know
(She didn't have a clue)
Is that Mary also had a horse
And a kangaroo,

An orangutan, an elephant,
An aardvark, and a leech,
A very hungry crocodile,
And Mary loved them each.

They followed her to school
Right into class, of course
(All were riding piggyback
Balanced on the horse).

Oh, the children laughed and cheered
To see these beasts in school.
They all thought that Mary
Was really very cool.

But friendships can be judged
By who rushes out the door
When it's time to clean the messes
Left lying on the floor.

Left lying on this classroom floor
Were messes very many
From all of Mary's animals.
Now friends, she hasn't any.

Three Blind Mice

Three blind mice, see how they run!
They all ran after the farmer's wife,
Who cut off their tail with a carving knife.
Have you ever seen such a sight in your life
As three blind mice?

Your wags have been chopped,
You poor little mousies blind.
Why did the lady cut 'em
Off your little mousie behinds?

Well, here is what her husband said;
He swore that it was true.
So exactly what he told me
I will tell to you:

She cut the tail off every mouse
"Because tails are useful round the house."
Often she would sweetly sing,
"A tail is good for anything."

"They're good for noodles, pickup sticks,
Good to tickle your toes,
Good for yarn, candlewicks,
Good to pick your nose.

"They're good for pickles, pizza topping,
Sprinkled onto stews,
Good for key rings, dental floss,
Good to lace your shoes."

But mousie wags soon weren't enough,
So she started chopping tails
Off of monkeys, off of tigers,
Off of hippos, off of snails,

Off of aardvarks,
Off of gooses,
Off of chickens,
Off of mooses,

And then one day she tried to chop
The tail off the end of a whale,
But he swallowed her up instead
And that was the end of *her* tale.

Little Jack Horner & Miss Muffet

Little Jack Horner
Sat in a corner,
Eating a Christmas pie;
He put in his thumb
And pulled out a plum
And said, "What a good boy am I!"

Little Miss Muffet
Sat on a tuffet,
Eating her curds and whey;
There came a big spider,
Who sat down beside her
And frightened Miss Muffet away.

Miss Muffet ran to her grandma's house,
Where she hid underneath the bed
And nervously ate her curds and whey
On pumpernickel bread.

But, alas, the spider had followed her,
And in fact, he'd almost swallowed her,
When out of the corner jumped Little Jack Horner
Licking his thumb (colored blue).
"What a good boy am I," said he,
And the spider he squished with his shoe.

Little Miss Muffet and Little Jack Horner
Soon grew incredibly fat
From a diet of curds and whey and pie
And caloric stuff like that.

The spider recovered and sued them both
For assault that was cruel and unfair.
Eventually he won the case
And now he's a millionaire.

Jack Sprat

Jack Sprat could eat no fat,
His wife could eat no lean,
And so between the two of them,
They licked the platter clean.

They licked the serving platter?
Their tongues all covered with spit?
They licked the serving platter?
How disgusting can you git?!

Their lickening was sickening
But it's what they loved to do.
"It's my very favorite thing," said Jack.
Said his wife, "Me too."

They licked the grand piano,
All of their children's toes.
They licked beneath the kitchen sink.
They licked their doggy's nose.

They licked the doorknobs, licked the chairs,
Licked the chimney flue,
Licked the goldfish, licked the stairs,
Licked every single shoe.

Soon they'd licked their house
Entirely span 'n spic,
So they headed out the door
For lickier things to lick.

They licked a city bus,
Licked a garbage truck.
They licked a boa constrictor,
A skyscraper, a duck.

And they would have licked forever,
They never would have quit,
But their licking days were ended
When their lickers ran out of spit.

I Had a Little Husband

I had a little husband no bigger than my thumb;
I put him in a pint pot, and there I bid him drum.
I bought a little handkerchief to wipe his little nose
And a pair of little garters to tie his little hose.

We had a little baby
No bigger than a flea.
We had to use a microscope,
She was so hard to see.

And a teensy-weensy tweezer
To change her little diaper,
And when her nose was runny,
We used fairy dust to wipe her.

We bathed her in a raindrop,
We dried her with a thread,
And we sang her fast asleep
In a daisy-petal bed.

We fed her crumbs of toast
And miniature pies
And the most exquisite milk
That we milked from butterflies.

She skated on a snowflake,
She jump-roped with a curl,
And she loved to play croquet
With an itty-bitty pearl.

At the age of adolescence, though,
Our darling little squirt
Quickly underwent
An awesome growing spurt.

Her size increased stupendously,
She ate us out of house and home,
And now our darling's bigger
Than a geodesic dome.

Bedtime

The Man in the Moon looked out of the moon,
Looked out of the moon and said,
" 'Tis time for all children on the earth
To think about getting to bed."

The Man in the Moon leaned out too far,
Grabbed at his windowsill,
Lost his grip, started to slip,
And took a terrible spill.

He fell to our planet, landed on granite,
And the shock of his terrible fall
Bumped poor old Humpty Dumpty
Off of the palace wall.